JOURNAL *of the* WESTBRAE LITERARY GROUP

Issue 1, Fall 2024

Berkeley

2024

ISBN 979-8-9917199-0-2

Published by Westbrae Literary Group
Berkeley, California

EDITOR
Jon-David Hague, Founding Editor

JOURNAL OF THE WESTBRAE LITERARY GROUP
Published semi-regularly by Westbrae Literary Group, promoting authors who bring fresh, raw voices to the forefront of American literature. We are dedicated to publishing work that challenges the traditional canon, offering a platform to writers with unique and authentic perspectives.

SUBMISSIONS
Westbrae Literary Group accepts rolling submissions year-round. We welcome work in the following categories: **Essays, Poetry, Art, Short Stories, Excerpts from Prose in Progress and Forthcoming**

Please submit manuscripts via email to submissions@westbraeliterarygroup.com. Include a brief cover letter and biography with your submission.

CONTACT INFORMATION
Westbrae Literary Group
info@westbraeliterarygroup.com
westbraeliterarygroup.com

CONTENTS

CONTRIBUTORS

Katja Bartholmess's life and creative work are fueled by a deep curiosity about people and their social and cultural dynamics. Growing up behind the Iron Curtain in East Germany, she began exploring the world after the fall of the Berlin Wall. After time in Berlin, London, Pretoria, Tokyo, and NYC, she now resides in Los Angeles, dedicating herself fully to writing.

Jonathan D Dyson is a lifelong fan of epic fantasy, inspired by Tolkien's works, which he now shares with his children. After two decades of global travels, he continues to explore stories, myths, and legends, immersing himself in the fantastical in all its forms.

Josh Greenbaum has been writing poetry and assorted prose-like stuff for decades, specializing largely in unpublished works. When not braving the streets of Berkeley on his bike, he can be found hiking, breathing fresh air, and cooking. He writes at the Left Margin Lit writers' workshop, where he is currently working on his first unpublished novel, an excerpt from which will be published in the next *JWLG*.

Ayana Sueishi-Hague is current working towards an animal technology degree and has been creating art from an early age.

Arthur Jackson V is a San Francisco artist inspired by music and language. Raised in the Bay Area, his storytelling blends raw honesty with influences from Erykah Badu, Jill Scott, and others, exploring the human condition through words and sound.

Liliana Hazel Navelgas is an English major at Westfield State University with roots in both New York City and Manila. She enjoys cooking, classical singing, and strength training in her free time.

James Rickman is an L.A.-based editor, writer, and musician. When he's not staring at a laptop, he's rockin' in the free world with the Cinnamon Boys, his Neil Young cover band.

Jessamyn Violet is a writer from Venice Beach, CA, with an MFA in Creative Writing from California College of the Arts. Her works include the poetry book *Organ Thieves* and the debut novel *Secret Rules to Being a Rockstar*. She is also the drummer of the band Movie Club.

Jay Youngdahl is a Southern lawyer, artist, and writer. He represents workers and unions, engages in "participatory action art," and has authored *Working on the Railroad, Walking in Beauty: Navajos, Hozho, and Track Work*. Jay is also an anti-war U.S. Army veteran.

EDITOR'S NOTE

Expression may be one of our most interesting evolutionary traits as a species, a trait unique to us. In our minds we can invent fantastical universes. We can plan out just about anything and run through scenarios to imagine how those plans might turn out. But none of these fantasies have to exist in reality, past or future, and none of us have visited any beyond our planet or the moon. Even fact must be expressed.

In the so-called West, with its own politics, culture, history, and influences — much of it originating from distinctly European ground — mimesis (μίμησις) is commonly referred to in the context of human expression and how we express. Aristotle made the word famous in his essay *Poetics*; it's often translated as "imitation," but to me that falls flat. "Reseeing" holds better. In our minds' eyes we *see* reality *again* and remake it in diverse ways through our expression. The contributors of this inaugural issue represent that.

Westbrae Literary Group as a publisher and its Journal place this "reseeing" in the context of our shared experiences here on the soil that bore us: geographically, physically, socially.

Where we "resee" matters.

Jon-David Hague
Berkeley, September 2024

POETRY

Santa Cruz, 1989

I have felt the earth so like an ocean's fury,
and I adrift on my own two feet.
I have known the awesome rush of sound and power,
blowing down the lives
the bricks
the books
that once lay stacked against the shockwave's grain.

I have seen poles dance, and cars rock back and forth.
I have seen the houses, oh beloved houses
that gave us home and cheer and warmth
now tossed in ruin on their littered yards.

I have smelled the quiet fear, the tense fear
the horror and the sadness that daily crowds our lives.
I have looked into the eyes of sorrow, of loss, of despair
those eyes all brimmed with tired lines and furrowed brow
and seen no hope.

Only survival, only confusion
only the dread knowledge that fate's cruel image
awaits in the background
of each bucolic scene.

I have opened my home, emptied my cupboard,
boiled water, cleared bricks, fought sleep,
comforted many, built lifelines, tried to laugh.
But mostly I sought to rebuild myself,

amazed at the stunning impact of mortality,
and the slight whiff of immortal life
that comes from surviving, oh this most trying life.

Now we live bewildered lives, cut off from routine
cut off from the past, the comfort, the knowing.
Our ruin is our isolation, our shattered lives
the new foundation for life's next shattering blow.

It's no longer just another rotten day in paradise.
For paradise, as we know it, was lost in a landslide
burned in a fire, tumbled in a shower of bricks and lime,
knocked from its moorings. and left without a home.

— Josh Greenbaum

Lost in my garden

One afternoon near the gate
In the back where a stream once ran
Its legacy two full commanding trees
Drawing that hidden water twenty feet into the sky.
The most formidable, a plum tree broad and tall like no other I've seen
And nestled half in its shadow of dark burgundy
A gentle willow,
Filling a fenced-in corner of the yard.

I strolled and filled a bag with rotten, half eaten plums shed from a height
Beyond any hope of harvest, at least by me.
It wasn't meditative, the cloying smell of rotting fruit
Made it very much a chore.
And yet I found myself lost among the trees
As I strolled under the dark rounded eaves of the willow
Living on the edge of a stream, as willows do.

Only this stream lay beneath us.
And as I listened,
I felt the rushing current's flow
Under my bare, plum-stained feet.
I paused, and then plunged in and was swept away.

— **Josh Greenbaum**

After Nostalgia

"If I had known, back then, you were coming… to save me after all"
— *"Against Nostalgia" by Ada Límon*

You've never met the person I was, you've never heard
the promise I made: I would bring color to my life
piece by piece. I would begin again.
Like in the Wizard of Oz, I suffered a storm, sacrificed home,
and I woke up to vivid rose, dandelion, venom.
What a journey I've had. If only I could remember
what led me to you: it's obvious, at first, to see
your arresting smile, to see it's all about you.
I wish I could say I've prepared for this, that I've run the film fully
and shown you what I was like when it was calm and mild.
I've set the past on fire. I've set it aglow again
and I will show you, I was someone before too,
I have the same walking legs you fell in love with,
I take the same steps that bring me to your embrace.
I dig for memory and it holds me up. Memory has completed me for you.

— **Liliana Hazel Navelgas**

clumsy me

I bump into things   like
      all the time
Corners   The night
        stands edge   my
        head
           against
                a wall

Clumsy little black boy
Never grasp the sand boy
Never wants the party to end boy

Always holds his breath
before pressing send
               Hold your breath
               Count to three

Letters always leave weird sugar on your tongue

The way they taste like the edge
                  of

                     leaving

You found me at the edge and called
my name like succeeding Mount Everest
We, nephilim

Red giants

only took two years to become nova

«I heard it takes two years come down from that
beautiful place; I heard it's so nice»

Was so bright and
All glow and heat

I knew needle and thread but   You
showed me so

            Lucky me

                        — Arthur Jackson V

<u>blow out the candles</u>

for John B.

I feel like my brain has been   put
on pause on stand by   I'm
waiting for shit to make sense.
I feel both
    piled
<u>on and swept</u>
under the rug

"Nothing ever lasts forever"

Remove the *ever* and it makes more sense
        Nothing is the longest relationship

The final girl
     Wooden stakes
       Esteem & strength
        And witty catchphrases

I thought that was me   I
was my stories pink opaque Buffy
Maybe I still am and THIS is the illusion
Am I being beaten by illusion?

Is life just illusion?
Am I in a chaotic
     DMT
     Coma locked
     Slumber sleep
        Am I asleep?
Life is but an dream and
He don't want me
        no more   Hard back!

My friend just O.D.'d

    And I wanna wake up from this dream   I can't catch my breath
    He took off the mask
    our kiss is gone gone gone. John
            Insecure lion pockets full of
          alphabet curves & acrylic paint

        Tell me! Why does love always stain
          when it's poured all over you?

I wish I could scrub the stretch
of death off of me   All
the grains John B. buried
underneath. Forever eulogized
in his Van Gogh brush strokes
white knuckling the brushes
Impasto to be loved; Opalescent light house

         Call all four corners
          of the storm *on me*
           Down on me
       Lie open wide. Four empty corners
        where four elements should be

        Why is stardust just swept
          under the rug?

        Premature blow of a candle
           O u t
        Should still be burning

                   — Arthur Jackson V

ESSAY

Jay Youngdahl

Feeling Weird in Fort Mac

As we flew from Edmonton to Fort MacMurray black and white toothpicks seemed to jut out of the lush green undergrowth below us, rising toward our plane. I thought northern Alberta would be mountainous, but looking out the window to the horizon, the hazy dark layers I saw were bands of smoke from the yearly forest fires, not ancient rocks. Summer fires are constant here. I could feel that I was getting closer to a planetary pole. When I do, my cocoon of life seems to slightly morph, which feels a little weird.

I was headed on a short trip to Fort MacMurray, Alberta, "Fort Mac," the epicenter of the oil sands. In an ecological battle of descriptors, environmentalists call this area the "tar sands." I cajoled an opportunity from the Carpenters Union to take pictures of people and objects who make the oil extraction possible. Chasing awe, I came to feed my restless traveling soul, and to see what working class life was like in the area known for the most polluting oil extraction in the world. The painter Paul Klee famously described his artistic process as "taking a line for a walk." I was taking my camera for a walk.

During the week of my trip all Americans who read what passes for news today, were bombarded with "weird." As with most global citizens today, I am addicted to my phone. Maybe attention to the phone screen made me ADHD, or maybe I already had the affliction. Maybe that is why I came to think as I do – constantly mentally interrupted, constantly connecting disparate matters. Like Billie Holiday, "I can't stand to sing the same song the same way two nights in succession." But through my iPhone this week, "weird" was having more than fifteen minutes of fame.

My phone told me that Donald said Kamala is "weird;" and that Kamala returned the slur. Their sidekicks, Tim and J.D., competed to invent new ways to define the "weird" of their opponents. Liberal media got into the act. The New York Times applauded the use of "weird" by their favored political side, calling it "deft, articulate, and possibly prophetic." The UK Guardian even wrote of the "weirdness" of Trump's suits. I guess it is politically important today to classify the clothes of your opponent as "weird." I always thought suits with padded shoulders and long red ties were a kind of normal business attire. I had some a few years ago, but maybe I am not sensitive enough to "weird."

WHAT DID YOU LEARN IN THE MEDIA TODAY?

In Davos in 2024, the playpen for the global deep state, the "meritorious," the Editor of the Wall Street Journal told the "Defending Truth" panel, "If you go back really not that long ago, as I say, we owned the news. We were the gatekeepers, and we very much owned the facts as well."

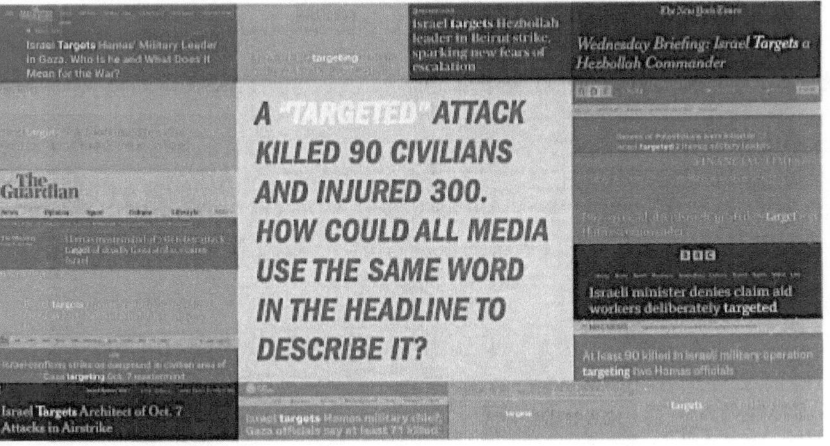

Some "weird" makes sense to me. The idea that the rules of physics which operate at a micro level are completely different than the ones which operate on our conscious life plane is unfathomable. Two things in the same place at the same time? Parallel universes? Maybe there really is a god of small things. A psychologist that my mother worked with had a theory he called "Dog Brain." Dogs cannot do calculus, he said, not because they are dumb, but just because they have dog brains. So maybe "weird" physics is something my human brain just cannot understand.

> *If you're not careful, the newspapers will have you hating the people who are being oppressed, and loving the people who are doing the oppressing. –Malcolm X*

"Weird" is a cousin of "surreal." Surrealism, defined as an artistic and political movement remains, but the descriptive use of it has lost all meaning. As we live through our phones, modern life does seem surreal; but if everything is surreal, is nothing surreal? The movie director James Cameron complained recently that it is almost impossible to write science fiction today as reality is already occupying the space.

In the lands below our plane, there is more potential oil than in Saudi Arabia, but it is costly to get to and difficult to refine. The most common method of extraction, honed in the coal strip mines of the American west, is to clear off a thin layer of dirt, clay, and trees from the boreal forest, to reach the sands below. The sticky sands contain bitumen, a kind of primitive petroleum. This thick substance is loaded into giant trucks and taken to go through a process to turn it into something like crude oil that can be shipped through large pipelines to Edmonton or more often to Texas, to be refined into the products we use.

No question: the burning of the fuel produced here contributes to climate change. No question: remediated, the land is scarred by the work. But it produces, as well,  an unrivaled source of working-class jobs, jobs which in contemporary Canada and elsewhere can support a lower middle class family lifestyle.

As our plane approached Fort Mac, the land looked like a scruffy face of one who had lived a hard life. A tattooed flight attendant strode through the aisle. Red isosceles triangles came out the tips of her fingers. Forming an acute angle at the top, they exuded a painful sexuality, in the style of Bella Thorne.

Noise was a feature of the trip, a discordant Fort Mac symphony. This was the first prop plane I had been on in years, and it was loud. At the scaffolding training centers, I visited aluminum rods being constructed into scaffolding constantly clanged, like the rhythms of a modern classical music piece. At holding ponds, shallow bodies of water used and polluted by the extraction and refining process, propane guns boomed to scare away wildlife.

PHAROAH SANDERS LISTENED TO NOISE

When I moved to Little Rock as a child, Little Rock native Pharoah Sanders was there as well. Poets loved Sanders. Amiri Baraka said that Sanders is a "consciousness in conscious search of a higher consciousness." The poet Harmony Holiday interviewed Pharoah Sanders once.

What are you trying to accomplish artistically at this point?
Right now, I don't even know myself!
Still? Do you feel like you've ever had a moment, or a record, where you've been, like, "I got this one right"?
No.
What do you listen to these days?
I haven't been listening to anybody.
Not even older stuff?
I haven't been listening to anything.
I listen to things that maybe some guys don't. I listen to the waves of the water. Train coming down. Or I listen to an airplane taking off.
Have you always been listening for sounds like that?
I've always been like that, especially when I was small. I used to love hearing old car doors squeaking…. Maybe it's something you're really into, then maybe you'll get a sound like that. I just wondered, Would that be a good sound?

Thousands and thousands of working-class men and women have worked in these sands over the last thirty years. Some who came to work in the

initial construction stayed in Fort Mac, but most took their earnings and returned to their homes. For years the main workforce was "Newfies," men and women from Newfoundland. Today an increasing number in the workforce comes from East Africa. "New Canadians" they are called. Earning solid working-class wages, they return home with a knowledge of this life and a pocket full of cash. I asked one African apprentice who was learning to be a scaffolder how he liked it. "I don't," he told me, "but I like the money." Worldwide, pockets of migration of laborers, whether Bangladeshi's building World Cup venues in the Middle East or oil workers here in Fort Mac, are a modern by-product of imperial plunder.

If you Google Fort Mac, you see harsh critiques

by environmentalists and non-native advocates for Native peoples, the First Nations. Much of the land being stripped is their land. But the relationships here are complicated. The struggles over the last decades have intermeshed many Native peoples into the capitalist economy. Today many tribes receive money from the tar sands. Once these financial flows begin, they are hard to turn off. While I saw few native people, their presence could be felt and seen throughout town. They own the hotel I stayed in, as well as many of the local services. The tribes provide buses that take oil workers back and forth to work from their "man camps," the stacked boxy structures built to house temporary workers.

As I had done in Edmonton, I was able to see the Fort Mac worker training centers for scaffolders. In the US, these workers often call themselves "scaffold dogs." Scaffolders build gleaming skeletons which

envelope commercial and industrial construction sites to be climbed on by other workers. Anyone who has been in NYC over the last decade knows all about scaffolding. In some areas of Manhattan you can walk for blocks, confined in a claustrophobic corridor of sliver pipes. Money must be changing hands there, as they never seem to be removed. Scaffolding brings money to Fort Mac too. Workers get paid a union wage to build these metal Lincoln log-like structures to protect the workers who work on the edifices and those who walk below. For Fort Mac industrial sites, under the scaffold the workers place "diapers" to catch whatever falls. Unlike in NYC, though, they take the scaffolding down when the work is over.

Talking with workers in Edmonton and Fort Mac many do the same work as their parents and their parents' parents. They remain working class. Maybe Lamarckism is owed another look. Characteristics we acquire during our lifetimes seem to pass to our kids, a kind of body memory that comes to reside in our genes. I had a hippy girlfriend once who believed that "the body never lies." It was fun to explore that concept with her.

Descriptions of the working class today are couched in "weird" political symbols. In the US the term "working class," is a disfavored term. When used politically, "working class," is often code for racist white men who are insanely trying to return to the mythical "good old days." In my experience, though, those who labor with their hands and bodies seek a humbler and more mundane path — to be able to live a life free from worry. When I was young and my father was a union organizer, we sang at home.

The Mill Was Made of Marble
Joe Glazer

The Mill was made out of marble, The machines were made out of gold. And nobody ever grew tired, and nobody ever grew old.

I dreamed that I'd died, And gone to my reward; A job in Heaven's textile mill, on a golden boulevard.

It was quiet and peaceful in Heaven, there was no clatter nor boom. We always had beautiful music, while we worked at the spindle and the loom.

There was no unemployment in Heaven, We worked steady all through the year. We always had food for the children, and we never worked in fear.

I woke from my dream about Heaven, And wondered if there would be, A Mill like that one here on Earth for people like you and Me.

And the Mill was made out of marble, The machines were made out of gold. And nobody ever grew tired, and nobody ever grew old.

The economy of a place determines so much. Some economies are cool, and some aren't. Fort Mac isn't, but all folks who use AI and need the energy sucking data centers, rely on uncool economies. Without the energy from places like Fort Mac, there would be no Chat GPT.

It is easy to criticize the economy in another place. I saw this in the San Francisco Bay Area, where I lived for much of the 2010's. I loved the attitude of Oakland, the city was filled with children whose parents came from Arkansas and Oklahoma to work after World War II. But today the economy there is centered around non-profits and tech. Jobs in these cool sectors provide the plethora of toys that a six-figure salary gets you in the Bay Area, but they produce the Ubers and "defense tech" which causes havoc throughout the globe. The professional managerial class of the Bay Area

UBER WEIRD

In Edmonton I took two Ubers. The "platform economy," in which workers get their orders from their phones is the height of "weird." Ten years ago wealthy leaders of tech built a movement, engineered by the liberal intellectual elite many of whom had worked in the Obama administration, to convince all that this platform economy would bring a freedom and a creativity that was needed after the Fordist economy. The founder of Uber, Travis Kalanick, told all "I believe in creating a workplace in which a deep sense of justice underpins everything we do."

It was a sham. In cities throughout the world, including Edmonton, being an Uber driver provides far less than a living wage. You have the flexibility to be poor. But in the current "weird" way that progressive art and slogans from the 60's are used by corporations, the CEO, Dara Khosrowshiahi, who earns over $50 million a year, tell us that "We don't believe in a world of us versus them; we look at the world as all of us together." Together, like in a feudal manor.

would shrivel without their jobs in private equity tech, financed by workers pension savings, and in non-profits which recycle the profits of the very, very wealthy. It is hard to trash the economy that provides your income. It is easy to disparage others though.

After I checked into my room in the Native owned hotel in Fort Mac, through the orange and gray sky I could see tips of golden arches jutting above the tips of the short boreal foliage. The town has the Burger Kings, McDonalds, and convenience stores that mark cookie cutter urban sites. Stepping out of the room into the hotel hallway the smoke from the forest fire mixed with the benzene from the oil production. Fort Mac speaks to many senses.

While in Fort Mac, through my union friends, I was fortunate to score a visit to one of the gigantic projects that produces oil from the sands. Here, steam is injected into the sand and oil is sucked out with giant straws. This method obviates the necessity to strip the earth. With either process, though, the oil heads south to power our non-green, "green" activities like generative AI and battery powered scooters.

My friends took me in their Ford 150 pickup out to the site. Men with trucks argue about Ford v. Chevy v. Dodge here just as the workers in the South do. We drove pass a Native convenience store. It had a sign on the door reading that abusers were banned from the store. I never learned which abusers they were cautioning. Along the road, beavers seem

unconcerned with human activity, building large dams, beaver apartment houses, in the ponds. There, I saw my first duck of the trip. While I had seen some crows from my hotel, this was the only other species I had seen in Fort Mac. I don't think birds like what humans have done to the area. But maybe it is the propane cannons that keep them away.

Leaving the refinery, I returned to the Fort Mac airport, which was full of oil workers. Once through security, every hour on the hour, a disemboweled voice reminds you that the airport sits on native land. As I walked to my gate, I had to run the gauntlet of consumerism that one sees in every airport today. It reminded me of the current iteration of "everything is for sale," and that everything is commodified. This weirdness runs from Fort Mac to Cambridge and New York. America's current hedge fund darling, Ken Griffin, has been essentially able to buy Harvard as well as the Whitney Museum of Art. The President of Harvard genuflected to Griffin's philanthropic millions, and in exchange, it renamed its school of arts and sciences for Mr. Griffin. Harvard, the president wrote, "has nurtured and expanded the ambitions of students who have changed the world through their vast and varied scholarly pursuits. Now, the Harvard Kenneth C. Griffin Graduate School of Arts and Sciences will do the same," Griffin was also able to buy part of the Whitney Museum of Art. Entering the museum foyer, now named Kenneth C. Griffin Hall, a neon art piece weirdly, and unironically reminds us that Griffin became so fabulously wealthy by exploitation.

Nearing my gate, some tie dye garments caught my eye. They were all stamped with "Oil Sands." The hoodie went for $40 Canadian, about the pay for an hour of work for a scaffold dog. I think Jerry Garcia would think they were "weird."

Prose
Short Stories

Katja Bartholmess

The Girl Ruby-Doux
A slightly creepy bedtime story

In the heart of Manhattan, a girl lives with her mother. The child's name is Ruby Dumont, but her mother affectionately calls her Ruby-Doux. They reside in one of those iconic skyscrapers whose tops look like someone took a sharp knife to a castle in Europe and grafted it onto a high-rise building.

"It's time," the mother, seated by her daughter's bedside, reminds her. "You have a big day ahead today."

At her mother's gentle touch, Ruby-Doux claps her blue eyes open. The expression on the mother's face, solemn before, transforms into a radiant smile that brightens her delicate features at the sight of the child awakening.

"A while longer?" Ruby-Doux asks, reluctant to leave her cozy bed, where she lies on her back, her long black hair like loose tentacles around her on the bulging pillow.

"It's time," the mother repeats, lifting the down comforter off her daughter as she, herself, rises to standing. Underneath the covers, the little girl is wearing a pair of embroidered damask bloomers that seem to harken from a different era, paired with a pink t-shirt encrusted with rhinestones and a Minnie Mouse print.

With a pout of reproach and her prominent forehead leading the way, Ruby-Doux follows the narrow silhouette of her mother down the lengthy corridor that leads from her room to the grand kitchen. In its center sits a table large enough to seat an orchestra. If you took the time, you'd count eleven vases, all filled with flowers, albeit none of them fresh. In some places, the dark ebony of the wood is blotched with white wax drippings from an assortment of candle holders.

Ruby-Doux clambers up on a wooden chair with clawfoot legs. Two stacked silken bolsters elevate the 5-year-old so she can reach the steaming porcelain cup her mother is placing on a crystal coaster in front of her.

The girl scrunches up her nose.

"What is this?" she asks.

"You know what it is," her mother replies, lighting a few pieces of yellow copal resin in a saucer. "You drink it every month."

As the scent of eucalyptus fills the air from the burning copal, Ruby-Doux's mother slides an earthen pot of honey toward her child.

"It's your nettle tea," she says. "Seasoned with lavender blossoms and cayenne."

With her small fingers, Ruby-Doux rotates the wooden honey dipper in the viscous, golden liquid to then plunge it into her cup. As she stirs, her gaze is fixated on her mother who sits at an angle from her.

After breakfast and bath time, the mother dresses her child in cycling shorts the color of an oil slick on a puddle and a starched cotton blouse whose Victorian collar and intricate lace patterns match her own. While Ruby-Doux fastens the velcro straps of her red Mary Jane sandals, the mother finishes her daughter's braids before grabbing a dog collar hanging from a hook by the entrance door.

And off they go!

An elevator ride, a train ride, and a ten-minute walk take them to their destination. "Can you read what the sign says?" the mother asks.

"A-N-I-M-A-L-H-E-A-V-E-N," Ruby-Doux deciphers, squinting as her pointer finger picks out each letter on the green awning above.

"Bravo," the mother praises. "Animal Heaven."

"That's the loveliest name, yet," the girl says just as the mother pushes the button labeled "Ring here!"

"We're here for our appointment," the mother announces.

The woman behind the counter takes one look at the mother and absently straightens her t-shirt, aware that her own frumpy attire stands in sharp contrast to the meticulously dressed woman and the peculiarly outfitted child.

"Yes," she says, running her finger down a printed list. "Elizabeth Dumont, you're here for a small dog?"

"That is indeed so," the mother confirms.

With Ruby-Doux's hand clasped a little tighter, they follow the shelter volunteer down a corridor lined with rows of crates on either side. Passing each crate unlocks a new bark until the

neon-lit space reverberates with a cacophony of them. The woman points out a few canines she believes might be suitable until she stops in front of the second-to-last crate on the right.

As she turns to face her two visitors, her eyes can't hide her enthusiasm.

"I have a feeling he might be the one," she says with a wink to Ruby-Doux. When she unlocks the crate, a white fluff ball of a Maltese shyly pads toward the gate.

The little girl crouches down and wiggles her fingers. The dog tentatively wags his tail, only to get a fright and scramble to the back of his crate with a high-pitched squeal.

Ruby-Doux looks to her mother, tears welling up in her blue eyes and her little mouth curling into a heartbreaking display of despair.

"I just don't want him to be scared of me," she whimpers.

But before her mother can respond, the shelter volunteer interjects, trying to dispel any doubt that this is the right dog for them.

"He's just a shy boy," she says to the child. "Don't take it to heart."

Addressing the dog, she says: "What is it, sweety? Is that a way to greet your new family?"

The mother gently lifts her daughter off her feet, placing her on her hip with practiced ease.

Once the paperwork is done, the mother retrieves the collar and leash from her purse, and secures them around the dog's neck before bidding their farewells.

As they stroll back to the train station, they pass a dog park.

"Do you want to let him meet the other dogs?"
the mother suggests.

Ruby-Doux, wrangling with the leash, gazes up
at her mother who stands with her back to the sun,
casting a shadow across her daughter's face.

"I suppose so," she replies, and together they
pass through the gate, stepping onto the wide
expanse of sand and grass.

The warm sun has stirred up the aromal of what
hundreds and maybe thousands of dogs have left
behind.

Ruby-Doux scrunches her nose.

"It smells like doo-doo," she remarks,
prompting her mother to start laughing behind
manicured hands. It sounds like crystal bells
ringing.

"Indeed, it does," the mother says.

As the girl unclips the leash, the small dog darts
away, pursuing a leisurely thrown baseball.

Her and her mother's eyes follow their new
dog's antics from the edge of the dog park as the
man who tossed the ball ambles over to them.

"This one's mine," he says, pointing to a lively
yellow Labrador. "Her name's Duchess."

The girl remains silent, only her mother slowly
turns her head and nods in acknowledgement,

absently twisting a silver locket hanging from a long chain around her neck.

When the man's dog snatches the ball and runs to return it, the white Maltese tries to catch up with her.

"Good girl," the man praises, retrieving the ball from his dog's mouth. It looks to be covered in the saliva of a whole pack of canines.

Not minding the grime, he stuffs the ball in his sweatpant pocket and kneels down to pet Ruby-Doux's dog.

"He seems like a real sweetheart," the man comments. "What's his name?" At that, Ruby-Doux fixes her eyes on the man who is now at her level.

"We don't give them names," she states simply, prompting a look of confusion. "Darling," her mother interrupts with saccharine cheer. "We don't say things like that."

Turning to the owner of Duchess, she says, "You wouldn't believe the things that sometimes come out of her mouth."

And with that, she swiftly takes the leash from her daughter's hand and attaches it to the white dog's collar.

"Well, it was delightful to meet you, but we have to be off," she says while the man rises to standing, his brow still furrowed.

He watches them for a moment, his hand scratching the back of his neck. When he calls out after them, mother and daughter have already reached the other side of the gate: "But what is the dog's name?"

The mother silently raises her arm in a wave and when she gives Ruby-Doux a nudge, the little girl lifts her hand as well.

As they step into the flow of people hustling down the sidewalk, they are out of sight within moments.

"That man was quite nosy," Ruby-Doux states.

"He was just being friendly," the mother explains.

Before they enter the train station and board the train uptown, the mother changes her mind and gets herself an espresso and a cup of frothed milk for her daughter.

Side by side, they settle on a green bench facing away from the sidewalk and street, overlooking a row of basketball courts where multiple pickup games are in full swing.

After savoring the last sip of her coffee, the mother rises to fill the empty paper cup at a water fountain and places it in front of the small dog. He eagerly laps it up.

"I'm feeling a little nervous about tonight," Ruby-Doux says, looking up at her mother, who immediately pulls her close and plants a kiss on her head — right where the hair parts.

"You don't need to be nervous," the mother reassures her. "You'll have the puppy." Ruby-Doux stretches her arms around her mother's slender waist.

"I know," the child sighs. "But not for the whole time."

On the train ride home, the white Maltese peeks out over the edge of the mother's purse, eliciting "Ooohs!" and "Ahhhhs!" from fellow passengers. He truly is an adorable dog.

As they step off the train, dusk starts to settle in. The mother quickens her step until Ruby-Doux has to break into a little jog to keep up.

Upon reaching home, they wash their hands and then the mother gently unravels her daughter's braids and combs out her hair with a wooden paddle brush.

"It's time," the mother then says, guiding her daughter who's holding the dog by the leash, down the long corridor until they stop in front of a wooden door.

She opens this door that looks like all the other wooden doors in this apartment. Except this one has a second door right behind it. It's more of a gate, really — fortified with metal bars.

Extracting a skeleton key from the locket around her neck, the mother opens the gate and guides her daughter and the dog inside. After a brief embrace she turns on her heels and locks the gate behind her.

Removing the dog's collar and leash through the metal bars, she looks at Ruby-Doux who has settled in the solitary chair in the room – similar to the claw-footed ones they have in the kitchen. When her daughter fixes her eyes on her mother from across the room, their bright blue starts to give way to an amber glow. At that, the mother flinches but quickly catches herself as she takes a deep breath, forces a smile and closes the second door.

Passing the entrance door, the mother hangs up the leash and collar. On them, a few strands of the new dog's white hair. And when you look closer, you'll see them mingle with hair of other colors. Black among them, and yellow — reminiscent of the dog Duchess they encountered in the park earlier that day.

In the kitchen, the mother brews a pot of pour-over coffee and sits at the table with her cup steaming in front of her.

When unsettling sounds waft over from the end of the corridor and start to fill the space, the mother places her elbows on the table and her palms over her ears.

She doesn't turn on the light. The only illumination comes through a window behind her, cast by a moon that's peeking out from between the buildings.

It looks so full tonight.

Fury of the Wind

I can't do it this time." One admitted to the other.

"What do you mean, you can't do it? Why is it different this time?" The other asked.

"I don't know. It's… it's just different, ok." The first replied.

"That's not going to be good enough. It's your job. You are almost done. There is only one left." The second persuaded.

The first glanced in the direction of the tree. At the end of a cliff, overshadowed by another, barren rock stretched up toward the sky. The roots of the tree, stretching out in all direction. It was not able to penetrate the slate and yearned for sustenance.

The second followed her gaze, "Please help me understand. Maybe I can say something to the boss. If he finds out, we will both get stuck here. You know the rules, no leaving until the job is done."

"I don't think he will survive the winter." The first responded.

"All the more to get this over with and head south. Think about the kites and surf sails…" The second persuaded.

"Have you no heart? That's the last one, and it's all he has left. I can't take that from him. It just doesn't feel right?" The first lamented.

"You are kidding. Right? He has been clinging to that cliff for nearly a century. His kind isn't supposed to live that long anyway. He is well past his years. How did he even take root there anyway? This is impossible," the second argued.

Frustrated, the first moved closer to the tree. "That's just it. He's a fighter. I have pummeled him relentlessly, year after year, and yet he always comes back. He sleeps through the winter, and then those leaves just start sprouting everywhere."

"It's infuriating," the second mumbled.

"I know!" the first huffed. "But somehow, I get it."

She stared at the lonely old tree, with its sizeable worn trunk. It was black all over, some from the shadows blanketing it, and some from lightning that had hit it once before. A stray bolt her boss had thrown out. The top half had long since fallen to the rocks below. She glared at the last leaf on its branches. Her feelings became mixed inside her. She hated the leaves but wasn't sure why. Though, she liked the tree and didn't understand that either. Anger and sorrow began to battle within her.

"What are you doing?" The second frantically asked, but the first did not respond. "You are starting to twirl? Why are you twirling? You don't have permission. You are going to get us in trouble! Stop!"

But the first did not answer; she was indeed twirling. Her extremities pulled in and twisted about with intensifying speed.

"You have to stop! This isn't going to help!" The second shouted.

"I can't stop! I won't stop!" The sound of the first burst forth like a freight train, her anger now winning out in the extreme. She grew to a terrible height from the ground, surpassing the higher cliff in a moment and rising up to be seen, to be feared.

The second looked on in horror as she tried to get away, but it was too late. She was being sucked in. Her strength added to the first until she was fully absorbed, and they became one. Now she understood the passion of the first and joined her sister in rage. Together, they grew in immensity, calling out for justice.

Their siblings heeded the call. They came rushing from near and far, around trees, under cliffs, and from the highest heights. The power of the family grew, twisting about, growing in one-mindedness, a singular resolve. When they had gathered, they looked down upon the tree, reached out gently, and plucked it up from the cliff's edge. Swiftly they pulled the tree in and escaped.

They tore the landscape in their haste. They had caught the attention of the skies, and they grew dark in anger. Flashes of lightning began to build within the clouds. They ran for it, making great speed. The lightning was fast and deadly, but their boss was slow. Even still, they could not go far without him.

"Look, down there!" Cried one.

"Yes, the spot by the lake, fertile soil!" Another chimed in.

The family of wind carried the object of their obsession quickly to the spot and gently set him down. Some of them immediately began to rush back to their duties, as the winds of the world could not be very long from their task. The balance of strength was fragile, maintaining life or preventing it.

"Where is the leaf? It is off?" the first cried out in anguish as the others began to leave.

"Here!" One shouted.

"Careful!" The unison chorus of siblings chanted.

The first gently took the leaf, coldly in her hands. She stared at the little leaf. With all the strength of her family, she could not prevent this. The second was all that was left and looked on sympathetically.

The first reached up through the branches and tried to reattach the leaf to the twig it had clung to. "It won't go on!" she began to weep. She blew hard against the tree, the moisture of her tears soaking the branches.

"No, it will not. They cannot." The second consoled her.

The first looked back, "But why?"

"Because they are leaves, we are the breeze, and they come from trees. That is all there can be." The second explained sullenly. She did not have the heart to tell her about the tree. What life was left in it was now gone too.

The first blew back and forth in his branches until she realized the magnitude of what she had done, and before her sister could do anything, she stopped moving. She dissipated and was no more.

Excerpts From
Forthcoming Prose

The Last Summer
Excerpt

The old man points the tip of his cane at a bench ahead.

"Let's sit there," he suggests.

They settle on a green bench away from the flower beds that frame the lawn behind the hospital where the girl has been receiving physical therapy. Esteban rests his black lacquered cane with its chrome lion's head between them.

As he pulls out a pouch and starts rolling a joint, the girl suddenly inhales deeply, her nostrils flaring as she searches for a scent that hangs in the air.

Esteban smiles up at her from the side as he grinds a few flowers of weed, using a small tool.

"It's the honeysuckle," he says, pointing to the flowering bushes framing the square. The girl nods, intrigued.

"Hold this," Esteban instructs, handing her the pouch.

He stands, grabs his cane and strides toward a nearby bush, leaving the girl holding his stash. She hesitates, but follows him with her gaze.

With a grin, Esteban returns, cradling a handful of blossoms.

"Look at this," he says as he lowers himself back on the bench. There are a handful of blossoms cupped in his hand.

He carefully lets the blossoms fall onto his knee, using his thigh as a makeshift table.

"You can get the nectar like this," Esteban explains, pinching off the bottom of a flower. The girl's critical look melts into delighted surprise when the man pulls out a delicate thread with a drop of clear liquid.

"It's delicious," he says, slurping it up.

He offers a flower to the girl. Her eyes widen as she tastes the sweetness.

"It's amazing," she says, and immediately reaches for another flower.

Esteban smiles as the girl's weariness melts away and resumes rolling the joint he promised her. She takes a hit, coughs lightly, and inspects it curiously.

"Joints are so funny," she says. "Such a traditional way to get high. I usually just get edibles from the bodega."

Esteban starts laughing.

"From now on, I'm calling joints the traditional way to get high," he says and takes the joint from her hands. He puts it between his lips, careful not to burn his thick and well-groomed mustache.

As the joint's starting to take effect, the girl starts laughing, and relaxes against the back of the bench.

Esteban seizes the moment to gently probe into the girl's story.

"So, what's the story behind the sleeve?"

The girl's laughter fades as she adjusts the blue compression sleeve. Before she speaks, she prepares another honeysuckle flower, licks it, and then shrugs her shoulders. "I fell out of a tree."

"That's unexpected," Esteban says, surprised. "I would've guessed a skateboard accident." A smile steals across the girl's face.

"Actually, I was training for emergencies," she says. "I heard this speaker on campus talk about climate change and societal collapse. He said it's not a matter of 'if' but 'when' and that we need to prepare ourselves because nobody else will."

The girl pauses.

Esteban listens intently, his body language open.

The girl continues speaking, gaining confidence.

"I started preparing with survival training," she says. "I've got supplies and skills. You can learn so much from these people posting videos. But I'm still anxious. It feels unfair, knowing what's coming and feeling like no-one cares."

"I hear you," Esteban says to encourage her to keep going. She does.

"That's why I'm training myself to become completely independent," she says. "I got a small generator from an online marketplace, enough water and cans of food for a couple of weeks and I found solar-powered lamps that can also charge my phone."

"Why were you in the tree?" Esteban asks.

"That's just part of my training," the girl says matter-of-factly. "You have to learn to sleep in a tree. That's really going to help when society has gone to hell and everyone is roaming the streets. Sleeping up in a tree is a lot safer than sleeping in a doorway. At least once you learn how not to fall out of it."

The girl leans back on the bench. Esteban relights his joint and takes a breath of it. The girl wiggles her fingers and he passes it to her.

She realizes that this is the first time she has shared these things with anybody. Nobody had cared enough to ask what this was really about. Like her roommate who ridiculed her over her generator and provisions.

The girl and Esteban look out onto the flowerbed-framed lawn in front of them. A gray squirrel with an extravagant question mark for a tail crosses the lawn with the sinus curve of its movement, oblivious to the "Keep off the grass" signs posted on all sides. "I'm sorry that you feel like you have no future and that nobody does anything to change that," Esteban says after a while.

The girl lets out a hum of acknowledgement and lifts her right foot onto the bench seat. Twilight is settling around them and the shadows, long before, are disappearing.

"I know this might feel as if this is the first time anybody has ever felt like you do. That there is no future to live for. But I relate to what you said more than you might expect from an old fellow like myself."

The girl turns her head to face Esteban, her brow furrowed, not understanding what he means. Esteban continues.

"When I was in my early twenties all the way back in the 1980s, me and everyone around me felt like we were marked for death. We felt rejected and neglected by society. Not just by governments but by our own families."

When the girl knits her eyebrows together tighter with every word he says, he realizes that enough time has passed for her not to be able to put two and two together without him getting more explicit.

"It was the dawn of what would become the AIDS crisis and I thought that my whole life was a ticking time bomb."

The girl's eyes widen in understanding.

"Just as I was starting to live my life as an out and trying-to-be-proud gay man, everyone around me – lovers, friends, my whole community – got sick and died. There was one week in 1988 where I went to twelve funerals. And we were all just babies back then."

He softly shakes his head to dispel these painful memories.

"Everyone was scared of us. We were even scared of each other. I cursed my fate and my timeline. Why did I have to be gay? And if I had to be gay, why couldn't I have been born a decade earlier and gotten all the fun and freedom before there was a four-letter word to be scared of."

The girl listens to him as he listened to her.

"Nobody was looking out for us either so we started our own survival training. For us it meant using condoms for safe sex, avoiding intimacy altogether, or going back into closets we had fought our way out of at great expense."

"Were you scared?" the girl asks quietly.

"Scared to death," Esteban admits.

"Luckily, I got caught up in a few of the AIDS activist groups that sprung up across the city at that time," he says. "It allowed me to be useful. I could use my art and my Spanish mother tongue to help educate people that otherwise wouldn't have had access to information to help them be safe and survive. It allowed me to feel like it mattered whether I lived or died. And I realized that I really wanted to live."

The girl nods at him.

He pulls out a card that says "Artist + Activist" under his name and phone number. The girl takes it and turns it in her hand.

"Are you going to remark that this is a traditional way to share contact information?" Esteban asks with a wink.

This stumps the girl into laughter.

"Maybe," she says, matching his smirk. "I could've just added you on social."

She pulls out her phone and carefully adds Esteban's card to the card compartment on its back, alongside her student ID and her debit card.

Ellie Delight
The Question

Excerpts from Venice Peach, *coming June 2025 from Maudlin House*

Ellie Delight

Step right up here, Pop Stars and Punkers…
Welcome to the Strangest Show on Earth.

I'm Ellie Delight, a former sex-bot that has been reformatted into the psychic ringmaster of the Venice Peach Freak Circus. You don't know about it because it doesn't exist yet. My original owner, mad genius engineer Ringo Blackstar, grew guilty using me strictly for pleasure and reformatted me with my own intelligence, throwing in a counter-cultural edge. Little did he know, I would come to use this counterintelligence to break free of him to create and run a highly illegal underground show of forgotten talents in today's future.

This includes specimens like the Venice clowns, live analog rock bands, gypsy fortune tellers, a classically beautiful bearded lady, a prophetic typewriter poet, a one-armed jazz pianist, mad magicians, jugglers, smugglers, and a few two-headed snakes.

And myself, of course—psychic tarot reader and ringmaster of it all on a most important mission: I have come from the future to show you what happens when you ask the wrong question on the wrong night in the right place.

But first, I need you to take everything you think you know about Venice Beach and forget it. Throw it away for this ride. The California circus-by-the-sea has never been a place that can be summed up in a few mind-bending films, wild shows, or gritty reads. Like all extraordinary characters, there's too much to know. Like how Venice has had five different piers burn down, and they used to drill for oil right on the beach. Or how the oldest bar in Los Angeles was right off the boardwalk and one of the original speakeasys during the Prohibition era, complete with underground tunnels to smuggle liquor inside. And maybe everybody knows the whole town was founded by a wacky tobacco tycoon named Abbot Kinney, who built the original canals and called it Venice with the vision that it would become the most beautiful and expensive vacation property in the country, but violent gangs took over for decades.

If you did know all of those things, you're probably a local. And you may consider yourself in the unofficial westside club, Locals Only, originally formed by the wildest surfers known as the Z-Boys and the original Dogtown skaters. These were the fearless locals who would surf the most dangerous waters through the burned-down pier ruins, and the skaters who would tear up such rugged abandoned swimming pools that it was a wonder and testament to their true talents that anyone lived to tell the tales.

But this story takes place in a very different Venice, a Venice that exists a little further in the future than you're familiar with yet. Therefore, it's best ingested after forgetting everything you think you know.

See, where I'm from on the timeline, the robots are busy fixing everything. On all sides. Human-made history is finally sick of repeating itself. The people will elect corrupt celebrities to govern no more. Scientists, physicists and engineers secretly gathered funding to develop a Presidential Edition Robot back while the last human president, reality television star George Fuckwad, was in office.

TBD 3000 had a stunningly effective campaign. The robot was said to be programmed with just the right software to restore the country to its original breeding ground for commerce and creativity, innovation and art. And so, the American people voted to hand over the reins to robots.

In reports from the White House, President TBD 3000 claims that things are, in fact, starting to improve since the damage done by Fuckwad and his cronies. There was both a civil war and a great recession to recover from, which is no easy task for any human or non-human. Progress in most areas ground to a standstill. We're not as far along in the future as you would think.

President TBD 3000 claimed to be incorruptible, un-hackable, and only wanted what was best for the numbers. What else could it want? It didn't have an ego to protect, a demanding spouse to appease, mistresses to be blackmailed by, or households to uphold. Hell, it didn't even have any bratty children to send to exorbitantly overpriced universities.

It just wanted to run things, and to run things right.

Oh yeah, and restore the Great American Dream.

No glitches, no guts, no glory.

But despite these promises, as a countercultural intel robot, I could still see cracks in the system. I could also see that there still wasn't a place for everyone in President TBD's programmed vision/version of the future. So, born from the grand tradition of the Venice Beach original boardwalk Freak Show, and using the original speakeasy's basement, I started to secretly collect and showcase every outlier the current robotic leadership had refused to recognize in its rebuilding algorithm. I thought it was a great idea, building an army of magical misfits—until one of them asked the wrong question on the wrong night in just the right place to change the course of the future forever.

All this carnival ride asks for is a clear palate.

And a taste for a little bit of everything.

The Question

The supermoon hung low over the limitless stretch of the Pacific, its reflection like a shattered plate over the churning waves. The wind's jagged grasp carved up the water, smashing it onto the shore in frothy spews. Seagulls hovered in the sky, shrieking, bobbing and fighting the invisible currents that crisscrossed the shoreline.

A strange and wonky energy tugged and pushed at all those wandering the Venice Beach boardwalk at dusk. Drifters and vagrants scattered in search of shelter. Robotic security scanned the souvenir shops as the owners shuttered their doors and windows, preparing for a tumultuous night of hot gusts blowing in from Santa Ana. Airborne grit and grime coated the heaping piles of abandoned technology piled up around trash cans, covered benches and turbo-tennis courts like dirty snow. Outside gyms and the silicone skate bowl grew littered with fallen palm fronds and feathers.

From an alley behind the boardwalk, a lone woman with her head wrapped in a silk scarf darted inside a juice and smoothie stand marked only with a spray-painted peach, just as the employee inside moved to lock the front door.

"I need to see Ellie," the young woman said. "It's an emergency."

The employee simply nodded as the woman moved past her and disappeared behind the door marked "EMPLOYEES ONLY." Inside the office, the woman punched in a code to the safe that prompted the entire shelf to swivel to reveal a set of narrow, dimly-lit steps leading down to what looked like a dungeon. She plunged down the stairs without any hesitation.

The underground Venice Peach Freak Circus was especially empty that night, with just a few Venice clowns who sat at the bar, sipping drinks dejectedly. Hunky, the one with the prison-striped ball nose and giant floppy ears covered with barbaric piercings, honked at the sight of her.

"Odessa! You're a sight for sore ears." He wiggled his huge, pierced-up ears.

"Hi, Hunky."

"What about me?!" asked the green-haired clown with a patchwork bodysuit of a million tattoos, wearing only a black leather loincloth.

"Hey, Punky. Sorry guys, can't chat right now."

She hurried on down to the end of the bar where their fearless ringmaster Ellie Delight sat at a barstool, wearing its trademark bejeweled top hat and suit, running the books through its own untraceable program.

"Sorry to interrupt," Odessa said breathlessly as Ellie looked up. "I saw something in my dreams, and I need to know if it's going to happen."

"It is not a good night to go peering into alternate worlds," The psychic ringmaster said firmly. "The portals are especially thin on windy supermoons. Even a slight tear can set loose total chaos between every existing dimension. Besides," it added. "I can sense something is off with both you and the universe right now."

"But this is an emergency. I have to know."

"Why do you need to know?"

"It could be life or death."

Ellie smiled grimly as it removed a deck of tarot cards from the inside pocket of the jacket. "My dear, it is always a matter of life or death. But I am going to indulge you because you are one of us, though sadly still so very human in your flaws. What is your question?"

Odessa leaned over and whispered it into the ringmaster's ear microphone. Ellie's face did not change as the androgenous humanlike robot lay out the cards in a wave formation.

"Pick one," Ellie said somberly.

Odessa reached over and selected a card with a shaky hand. Ellie turned it over.

It was The Fool.

At that exact moment, there was a crack of thunder so loud it sounded like the place had been bombed. The lanterns flickered over the bottles behind the bar. The one-handed jazz pianist fisted the low end of the baby grand piano onstage. The clowns honked and hawed from their barstools.

"I'm afraid you should have stayed home this evening," Ellie said darkly.

"Why?"

"Your foolish question has summoned superdoom on the next supermoon."

Odessa's eyes widened. "For just me?"

"For us all. Now GO HOME, Odessa."

"I'm so sorry, Ellie." Odessa bowed her head, a tear running down her cheek. The ringmaster just waved Odessa off and closed its eyes.

As she hurried to leave, the prophetic typewriter poet handed her a slip of paper.

"Take this," they said.

"What is it?" Odessa felt a shock of electricity run through her as she took it from their slender hand.

"A transmission from the supermoon," they replied, peering up at her with wide eyes through wire-rimmed spectacles. "It just came in. I think it's for you."

She folded it into her pocket and braced herself for the windy walk home.

James Rickman

You Are Not at Home

excerpt from forthcoming memoir Run Screaming

We hadn't heard of most of the towns we played. We were an eight-piece ska band from a small beach town in California, trying to stay afloat at the outset of the 21st century, two years after most of the world had turned on ska, and we were a week into our first tour of the U.K. and Europe. We played clubs, pubs, squats, and, in Erfurt, Germany, an actual dungeon with vaulted stone ceilings, where the soundman kept asking us, "You want fuck machine?" until we realized he was asking about the *fog* machine sitting sidestage.

We crossed the Channel to Belgium on a mid-September afternoon, and as we rolled off the ferry our English driver told us that the first order of business was to secure several orders of pommes frites with pindasaus—a thick, copper-colored goo that tasted like melted JIF peanut butter mixed with curry powder and a dash of vinegar. We were skeptical until we received our frites, served in steaming newsprint cones, and took our first saus-heavy bites, and then we were addicted. Hours later, after we'd played our show and met a quiet college student who offered to put us up at his apartment, we smoked some very strong weed, which made us murderously in need of more frites.

Our host offered to make a run to a late-night chip shop, and I joined him. I seldom smoked, because weed almost always made me paranoid (that the music was too loud, that I had said and then immediately forgotten that I'd said something inappropriate, that I had permanently fucked up my brain, etc.), but that night I had taken some hits off the professionally rolled, cocktail carrot–sized joint that some of the band was passing around, and I got very stoned. As we walked the quiet streets, our host struggled to speak English, as did I. By the time we'd arrived at the chip shop, I was on about a six-second delay. He placed our order and we leaned against the wall opposite the counter, behind which two lean young men in T-shirts and bandanas worked the fryer. I noticed that our host was talking.

"Why did you stay with me?" he asked.

The question surprised me, and I could barely hear my own voice, but I tried to explain. "Well, we stay with people who come to our shows pretty much every night, even if we've never met them before. Without cool people like you, we couldn't afford to tour."

"Yes, but…" He looked down and crumpled his brow. "But you could have stayed with someone else."

It was hard to get his meaning with all the alarms going off in my head, but I sensed acute loneliness tinged with resentment, as if the guys currently stinking up his apartment were just humoring or using him. Maybe there was some truth to that, but I tried to beat it back.

"Yeah, but, really, it's the generosity of people like you that keep us going," I said. "And also, meeting people is like the best thing about touring."

Now I heard another voice: one of the guys behind the counter, who was looking at me with his chin raised.

"American?" he asked.

"Yeah!" I said, praying for some smalltalk to lighten things up. Maybe this frites-man had been to America, or his favorite band was American. Maybe his favorite band was us!

Then I saw the face behind the counter go hard. With a suddenness and volume that almost made me lose control of my bladder, he barked,

"Fuck you and die!"

*
**

Den Helder, our next stop, is a port town at the northern tip of the Netherlands. It's tiny but, just as we had hoped, it had a shabby little strip lined with "coffeeshops," where there were actual joints under glass counters and hazy, dorm-like lounges, each one piping Bob Marley's *Legend* through small speakers. Our show was to take place at a dank bar open to a narrow street. We set up and met a few people, unable to distinguish staff from regulars. A sweet-faced man with long hair invited us to his house, just around the corner, where we could make tea and listen to records until gig time. With many hours to kill and few options besides getting baked, three of us accepted.

The man led us down the road, and I asked him about life in a country where everything was legal. In solid English, he replied that he had recently stopped taking drugs. So we became deeply confused about ten minutes later, when we found ourselves sitting across from him in a dark, cluttered living room while he poured white powder onto a small circular mirror. He had just put on an Maceo Parker live record, very loud, and he chopped and snorted the powder at the beginning of a wild saxophone solo that kept modulating upward, one half-step at a time. He had to shout to be heard, and shout he did, mostly a congested "YEEEAAAAAH!" as the solo kept twisting and stabbing its way up. We sat shoulder-to-shoulder at our end of the coffee table, catatonic, wondering how we would ever get out of there. Outside, the sun was still high in the sky.

Several hours later, about thirty people watched as we played every song we knew against the back wall of the bar. There was no stage, so the band kept spilling into the crowd and vice versa. It was easy for the guy dancing directly in front of me to pour beer into my mouth while I tried to sing; muscular and square-jawed, with a blond flattop, he reminded me of Guile from Street Fighter II, if Guile did a lot of cocaine. We sensed that everyone at the show knew each other—and sure enough, when we got to the apartment where we were to spend the night, pretty much the entire crowd was there. Most of them were zonked on something. Our driver sat next to a guy whose eyeballs pulsed and whose toes were torqued upward inside his shoes, which took the shape of hockey sticks. He made halting smalltalk and, during lulls, puffed out his cheeks and went,

"*Dvvvvvv*," as if mimicking the sound of a vacuum cleaner.

I started talking to a woman in a black dress and heavy black eye makeup. Her English was good and she didn't appear to be high, although judging by her calm and her quiety sardonic tone she was well accustomed to people who were. I liked her; also, I was drunk and tired and grateful for a break from the many incoherent conversations I'd had with zonked-out locals. I had no idea whether she was one of the apartment's tenants, but we stepped inside a tiny bedroom, switched off the light, and made out clumsily in a single bed next to the door. The party went on for hours, with frequent blasts of light and noise as people barged into the room.

Meanwhile, Josh, our keyboardist, found another bedroom and sacked out. He awoke to the feeling of someone mounting the bed. Opening his eyes, saw the silhouette of a large man holding a pointy object over his head. Josh tried to get up, but he was pinned. The man spoke.

"*You are not at home!*"

He brought his hand down, and Josh saw that it held a ballpoint pen. Then the man's face came into focus: It was Cocaine Guile. He gripped

Josh's upper arm and began to write on it. Then he hopped up and left. Josh turned on the light and found the word HOLLAND neatly inked on his bicep.

Finally, the party died out and the rest of the band found a room or corner in which to get a little sleep. The next morning we dragged ourselves back down to the street. I hugged and probably said "see you around" to the girl in the black dress; we had spent far more time writhing around together than we had getting to know each other.

As the days rolled on, the band made some generalizations: Ska shame had not spread across the Atlantic; here people skanked as sweatily as we had in America at the other end of the decade. Things were overall looser, which explained why some of us were having more romantic encounters than usual. And as Americans we inspired a lot of derision and hostility (*fuck you and die!*), but it was worth it for the blanket curiosity. None of this meant that we were packing houses, although we were very happy with the fifty to one hundred people who came out most nights, and, for reasons sketchily explained by our promoter on faxes and venue answering machines, shows started getting canceled—seven in all.

This gave us lots of time to meet new people and run out of money. In Utrecht, our driver hooked us up with some squatters who had taken over a warehouse near the red-light district. We got fed at a long picnic table and watched some punk bands play in an adjoining live room. That night I bedded down on some scaffolding, great gaps open to the ground floor 20 feet below, listening a song that kept repeating "Death to everyone is gonna come" on my Walkman.

If Roth, Germany, has a downtown, we didn't see it. Our show was a at country inn with a large live room and an upstairs apartment that was overrun almost as soon as the venue's doors opened. The rooms where we had tucked our bags were suddenly full of kids getting wasted, some of them using a MacGyver-like contraption I'd never encountered: a two-liter plastic bottle, its bottom half cut off and a metal carb poked into its flank, partly submerged in a bucket of water. I watched as they took turns putting their mouths around the bottle top, filling the bottle with smoke, and pushing it into the water, thus forcing a liter of solid white into their bodies. This, I learned, was a gravity bong.

That night we played one of our better-attended shows on the tour—maybe 200 people. The energy on the dancefloor lurched from happy skanking to heckling and weaponized elbows. We didn't mind (or understand) the German jeers, but there were some brawny skinheads getting aggressive up front. After the show I was ordering a drink at the bar when one of them appeared beside me—beside and *above* me, my head reaching his bare, cryptically tattooed shoulder. In broken English, he explained, I think, that he and his friends weren't bad skinheads. He got us a round of Jägermeister shots and, because it took a long time to explain the complexities of skinhead culture in a second language, he had time to order us two more. He was friendly—so friendly that he invited me to a party. I thanked him and explained that I had to stay with the band.

"Maybe I hit you on the head and *drag* you to party," he said.

How I laughed! We were having such fun, doing Jäger shots and razzing each other like a couple of old pals. He added,

"Maybe I pent your face."

...which I really didn't understand, and my nervousness was starting to show. I stammered that I had to go check on merch. Then I glanced up and felt our eyes lock, in the way that your eyes can lock with a feral dog. His features went still. Time seemed to slow as he bent and brought his face to mine, but it didn't slow enough for me to recoil. I had just enough time to wonder if this large skinhead was about to kiss me.

He put his mouth around my nose and bit. Not hard; just a playful chomp, and then he was back in focus and I was jogging to the merch table wiping Jäger-spit off my face.

Two days later, hanging out in Nuremberg, where yet another show had been canceled, a young couple who were letting us stay at their apartment invited us to a club night. Most of the band was worn out from an intense soccer match against a local pub team whose members had come to our last show. A band of messy-haired Americans in jeans and T-shirts took on a team of muscular Germans who'd shown up in spotless uniforms, and whose friendly ribbing turned icy once we started scoring goals. When our lead grew to three points we started to sense that, if we won, we would not make it out of Nuremberg alive.

So only three of us accepted our hosts' offer, and at sunset they led us into the heart of town. It was Oktoberfest, apparently: We crossed through a great plaza rammed with food stalls and long benches full of traditionally garbed revelers, and I got to pee while standing shoulder-to-shoulder with a large man in lederhosen.

The club, dark and boomy, could have been the gymnasium of a long-abandoned school. We got there early; no one was dancing to the soul obscurities blasting out of giant old speakers. Some of the people at the bar noticed us and smirked. The shirt I was wearing, a tiny red tee with NEBRASKA printed across the chest, probably didn't help. I walked to the bar—and ran straight into the nose-biting skinhead of Roth.

He was sitting alone, and although he smiled and reached out his hand when he saw me, he seemed a little subdued. Surely his buddies were en route, and once they got into the Jäger he'd be his nose-biting self again. Either way, I felt strangely happy to see him. If anyone decided to smack our stupid American smiles off our faces, my skinhead friend would come to the rescue.

My bandmates and I had some drinks, and we danced. The floor filled. The DJ was hot. Who knew there were so many great soul songs we'd never heard? No mashups, no beat matching, just one two-and-a-half-minute scorcher after another. I swayed, stamped, and waved my arms above my head. Hours in, I headed down a crowded corridor to the bathrooms, slipped on a beer puddle, did a bicycle-kicking leap, and landed on my tailbone. I clambered up the side of another large skinhead.

"*That* was embarrassing!" I said, and kept walking.

I noticed some posters taped up every ten feet—our tour posters, with the details of our canceled show scrawled on the blank part at the bottom. There I was, in grainy black-and-white, gripping a mic in one hand and holding the other straight up. Wearing my Nebraska shirt.

I doubt anyone at the club made the connection. But between the posters and my nose-biting friend and the pounding music and my sweaty bandmates and the beautiful girl in the red sweater who, at the end of the night, tried to teach me how to speak a complete sentence in German, I was glad our night had gone this way.

*
**

We went as far east as Vienna, turned around, and played a handful of shows across Switzerland and France. By then I had a cold; I bought some French decongestant tablets, and that was the closest I ever came to doing speed. On the remaining days off, we sought out Formule 1 hotels, which were 100 percent automated: no front desk, no overnight staff, just tiny, modular rooms like sleeping quarters in a low-rent *Space Odyssey*. After arriving at a venue that turned out to be a fitness studio, where some kind of French Jazzercise session was in progress, we were told by a man in a black leotard *"Pas de concert!"* The local promoter didn't speak English and so could not explain the cancelation, or why were were booked at a fitness studio in the first place, but he did lead us to a deserted country manor full of dusty leather couches, porn DVDs, and other bro-amenities. I was genuinely worried that I might open a door and find an obscure country scion's desiccated body on the floor.

We took the ferry from Calais back to Dover, crowding into a cell-like dormitory in the bowels of the ship. A week later we'd be back home, taking up whatever provisional jobs we had and trying to figure out how to keep going despite the mounting demands of adulthood and plummeting popularity of ska. I had been handed a bachelor's degree in English lit that summer, and I had moved back to my mom's house with absolutely no plan outside of the band.

But that would come later. Once the lights were off in that berth, we sank into the deepest darkness, and then the deepest sleep, I've ever known.

www.ingramcontent.com/pod-product-compliance
Lightning Source LLC
Chambersburg PA
CBHW030011010826
48973CB00009B/2756